with fund
by th
port Oui
sp

Switch Play!

Matt Christopher®

Text by Stephanie Peters

Illustrated by Daniel Vasconcellos

LITTLE, BROWN AND COMPANY

New York ∽ An AOL Time Warner Company

First Edition

The characters and events portrayed in this book are fictitious.
Any similarity to real persons, living or dead, is coincidental
and not intended by the author.

Matt Christopher® is a registered trademark of
Catherine M. Christopher.

Library of Congress Cataloging-in-Publication Data

Peters, Stephanie True.
    Switch Play! / Matt Christopher ; text by Stephanie Peters ;
illustrated by Daniel Vasconcellos. — 1st ed.
        p. cm. — (Soccer 'Cats ; #9)
    Summary: When Ted's twin sister Lisa, a fullback on the 'Cats
soccer team, gets attention for her special move on the field, Ted
determines to come up with an outstanding play also.
    ISBN 0-316-07650-3 (hc) / ISBN 0-316-73807-7 (pb)
    [1. Soccer — Fiction.   2. Self-perception — Fiction.
3. Sibling rivalry — Fiction.   4. Brothers and sisters — Fiction.
5. Twins — Fiction.]   I. Vasconcellos, Daniel, ill.   II. Title.

PZ7.P441833 Sw 2003
[Fic] — dc21   2002035918

            HC: 10   9   8   7   6   5   4   3   2   1
            PB: 10   9   8   7   6   5   4   3   2   1

                        WOR/CWO

            Printed in the United States of America

For my great-grandson,
Travis Chamberlain Howell

Soccer 'Cats Team Roster

Lou Barnes	*Striker*
Jerry Dinh	*Striker*
Stookie Norris	*Striker*
Dewey London	*Halfback*
Bundy Neel	*Halfback*
Amanda Caler	*Halfback*
Brant Davis	*Fullback*
Lisa Gaddy	*Fullback*
Ted Gaddy	*Fullback*
Alan Minter	*Fullback*
Bucky Pinter	*Goalie*

Subs:

Jason Shearer

Dale Tuget

Roy Boswick

Edith "Eddie" Sweeny

Chapter 1

It was a hot day on the soccer field, but that's not why Ted Gaddy was steamed. For the past minute, he'd been watching his fellow Soccer 'Cats cheer for his sister, Lisa. Both he and Lisa played the position of fullback. Both were good players, but Lisa had a special move that no one else on the team could do.

Whenever the ball bounced over the sideline near her, it was her job to throw the ball back into play. Most players did the usual two-handed, over-the-head throw. Not Lisa.

She was short and couldn't throw it very far that way. So she learned to do a front handspring throw-in. She actually would do a flip while holding the ball! When she finished the flip, she'd let go of the ball. It usually flew high and far into the air, way over most defenders' heads.

This move was her secret weapon. She didn't do it all the time. But when she did, it was a real crowd-pleaser. Today, Lisa flip-threw the ball to striker Jerry Dinh, who then made a goal. Even though Jerry was the one who had scored, it was Lisa who got most of the applause. As usual.

Ted knew he should be happy. His team was ahead of its opponent, the Panthers. His only sister—his twin, no less—had made it happen. But all he could think of was how no one had ever cheered for him the way they were cheering for Lisa.

The Panthers and the 'Cats got into position

to restart the game. At the whistle, the Panthers' center striker toed the ball to his teammate. The teammate quickly passed it back and the attack was on.

'Cats halfbacks Dewey London and Bundy Neel double-teamed the Panther with the ball. The Panther tried to pass the ball to his teammate. Amanda Caler, the third 'Cat halfback, jumped between them and stole the ball. Suddenly, the 'Cats were the ones on the attack.

Great, thought Ted, kicking at the grass. *Now we have to stand around again, waiting for the ball to come to our end.*

Usually Ted liked his position at fullback. He liked knowing that he helped prevent the other team from making a goal. But today, most of the action had been in front of the Panthers' goal. He, Lisa, and the other two fullbacks, Alan Minter and Brant Davis, hadn't gotten much action.

He watched Bundy battle for control of the ball with a Panther striker. Bundy won and kicked the ball back into Panther territory. The 'Cats fans applauded loudly.

I bet if I played halfback, people would clap for me, too, Ted thought sourly. *Or striker,* he added to himself as Stookie Norris scored a goal, his second for the game. Once again, cheers rang out from the stands.

But fat chance of that happening. It'd take a miracle for me to find myself in front of any goal but this one!

Stookie's goal was the last one of the game. When the ref blew his whistle a minute later, the 'Cats had won, 3–1.

After he'd shaken hands with the Panthers, Ted sat on a bench and took off his shin pads and cleats. As he was putting on his regular sneakers, Lisa sat next to him.

"Another win! Yahoo!" she crowed as she changed her shoes.

Ted was about to say something when one of the Panthers stopped in front of them. She was grinning.

"Hey, Lisa! When are you going to teach me how to do that flip-throw?" she asked. "It is so cool!"

Lisa grinned back. "Maybe when the season's over," she said. The girls laughed and the Panther walked away.

Ted rolled his eyes.

"What's that look for?" Lisa asked.

"Nothing," said Ted. He slid from the bench and started walking. "Let's just go home, okay?"

Silently, Lisa followed him. Ted could feel her eyes on his back, but he refused to turn around.

Let her see what it's like to be ignored, he thought meanly.

Chapter 2

Two days later, Ted showed up at practice still in a bad mood. He hadn't said much to Lisa since the game, and she'd given up trying to talk to him.

Coach Bradley called everyone together. "Okay, we'll do the usual passing and dribbling drills to start," he said. "Then we're going to work on something called switching. Switching is when a player changes positions with another player during a play."

He paused to make sure everyone was paying attention. "Now you all know the importance of staying in your own position. If all the halfbacks crowd the left side of the field, then the right side isn't being protected. If all the strikers go for the ball at the same time, then there's no one to pass the ball to. And I don't have to tell you what could happen if the goalie's out of position!"

The team laughed.

The coach went on. "Sometimes, though, it's a good idea to switch positions. Here's an example. A halfback has the ball. He wants to pass to a striker, but all the strikers are covered and can't get free. The halfback, on the other hand, has a clear field in front of him. It makes sense for him to keep control of the ball since he can bring it farther down the field, maybe into scoring range. So he switches with the closest striker by yelling that player's name and 'Switch!' The striker then drops back to the halfback's position and the halfback moves ahead into the striker's spot. Any questions?"

Bundy raised his hand. "When do they switch back?"

"Never!" said Jason Shearer in a spooky voice. "You're doomed to be a striker or a halfback for the remainder of the season!"

"Mr. Shearer," the coach said over the team's laughter, "kindly —"

"I know, I know," said Jason. "I'll kindly keep my jokes to myself."

"To answer your question, Bundy," Coach Bradley continued, "the players switch back as soon as it makes sense. That may be when there's a break in play, or when the ball changes direction toward the other goal, or when both players are close enough to each other to switch back to their usual positions."

He put a foot on a ball and leaned on his knee. "Let me stress again: It's important to stay in your own positions. But switching can be very helpful." He smiled. "I remember a time when I was playing in high school. A fullback on my team got the ball. He looked to pass it to the halfback on his side of the field, like he was supposed to do. But the halfback had just collided with the other team's striker. Both were down on the ground. Everyone else was covered, so the fullback started dribbling down the sideline. The halfback was still down when the fullback reached him, so the fullback switched with him and kept going."

The coach started chuckling. "The fullback crossed the center line and was about to pass it to the striker in front of him when the striker tripped on his untied shoelace and fell flat on his face! The defender had to leap over him so that he wouldn't fall too. The fullback kept going until suddenly he was in front of the goal! He did what any sensible player would have done. He took a shot."

Ted had been listening to the story raptly. "What happened?" he cried.

The coach sighed. "He missed and we lost the game. But the point is, he knew what he was supposed to do and he did it. And that's

what this practice is going to teach you—
what to do and when and how to do it. Are
you ready?"

Ted shouted "Yes!" along with everyone
else. His mind was spinning.

*If I could do what that fullback did — but score
instead of miss — I'd really wow the fans!*

Chapter 3

Ted could hardly wait to get the regular drills over with so he could learn more about switching. When it finally came time to practice switching, he found out it was pretty easy.

The coach split the team into two groups of five and sent Bucky Pinter into the goal. He called the first group up and used them to outline the drill.

"We're going to go three-on-two. Stookie, Bundy, and Alan are on offense. Stookie, you go about midway between the center line and the goal you're attacking. Bundy, line up about twenty feet behind him. Alan, you're twenty feet behind Bundy." The boys took their positions.

"On defense will be halfback Amanda and fullback Lisa. The defense will just stand there for now, until the offense gets the idea." Amanda placed herself next to Bundy. Lisa went between Stookie and the goal. The coach tossed the ball to Alan.

"Alan, start dribbling." Alan did. "Now usually Alan would pass the ball to Bundy, who would pass it up to Stookie. But this time, Alan, keep the ball and switch positions with Bundy." Alan continued to dribble slowly until he was next to Bundy. Bundy faltered, looked at the coach, then took a few steps back.

The coach held up his hand. "Whoa! Alan, you forgot to let your teammate know what you wanted to do. Unless you yell 'Switch!' Bundy's just going to think you're crowding his position. Try it again."

Alan returned to his position. When the coach blew his whistle, Alan dribbled toward Bundy. "Uh, switch," Alan said as he drew near. The coach's whistle shrilled.

"Louder, Alan," he advised. "Remember, it's going to be noisy during a game. You have to be sure your teammate hears you. Plus, a good loud bellow can surprise the opposition just enough to throw them off balance. And don't forget to say your teammate's name."

Alan tried again. "Bundy, switch!" he yelled. Bundy dropped back, allowing Alan to keep dribbling forward. When the coach didn't stop him, he kept going until he was near Stookie. After a quick glance at the coach, Alan yelled, "Stookie, switch!"

Stookie moved back. Suddenly Alan was in front of the goal. With a grin, he popped a short kick that sent the ball over Bucky Pinter's outstretched hands and into the net.

Ted bounced on his heels. He couldn't wait for his turn!

Chapter 4

Coach Bradley gradually made the drill more difficult. First he had Amanda and Lisa cover their players but not try to take the ball. Then he had them work harder and try to steal the ball. Finally, he told the offense to switch only part of the time to see if they could trick the defense. Sometimes it worked, sometimes it didn't. But after ten minutes, the first group had become used to yelling "Switch!" Now it was the second group's turn.

Ted was the fullback on offense. He, Dewey, and Lou Barnes went through the easy steps of the drill without a problem. Ted was eager to move on to the more difficult ones, when the defense would try to get the ball.

When they did, however, Ted ran into trouble. He yelled "Switch!" every time instead of mixing it up. So by the fourth time, Dale Tuget, the halfback on defense, was all over him. Coach Bradley blew his whistle.

"Ted, part of the point of switching is to catch the defense off guard," he reminded. "Try it a few more times, but keep Dale on his toes."

Ted did. He reached the goal twice, but the other times he lost the ball or was forced to pass. Still, those two times were enough to convince him that during a game, he could go all the way. In fact, he was determined to try it the very next game.

Three days later, he got his chance. The 'Cats were up against the Tadpoles. The Tadpoles weren't usually a very difficult team to beat.

Ted decided they'd be the perfect opponent for his switch maneuver.

The 'Cats won the coin toss and got the ball first. Ted watched eagerly as Stookie passed the ball to Jerry. Ted found himself hoping the 'Cats would lose control of the ball to the Tadpoles.

C'mon, get down this end, he wished silently.

His wish was granted five minutes into the game. The 'Cats scored an early goal and the Tadpoles took control at the center line. For once, their strikers easily passed the halfbacks. Suddenly, they were right in front of the fullbacks.

Ted and Lisa rushed the ball. Jabbing wildly with their feet, they managed to free it from the attacking Tadpole. Ted swept down on it and began dribbling downfield.

"I'm open!"

Ted glanced up and saw Dewey waving to him. Ted hesitated. His instincts told him to pass. But he fought back the urge and kept dribbling. Moments later a Tadpole halfback was on top of Dewey. Now Ted couldn't pass even if he wanted to!

"Dewey, switch!" Ted yelled. As he flew by, dribbling madly, he caught Dewey's surprised look. *But the Tadpole looked even more surprised,* Ted thought with satisfaction. He risked a quick glance over his shoulder to see if the Tadpole were chasing him.

Wham! Ted smacked directly into Stookie. The two boys tumbled to the ground. The ball bounced over the sidelines.

"Are you crazy?" Stookie bellowed. He scrambled to his feet and watched as a Tadpole threw in the ball over his head. "I was wide open! Why didn't you pass it?"

"Sorry," mumbled Ted. "I switched with Dewey and —"

"Yeah, well, you better switch back, pronto!" cried Stookie. "Look!"

Ted looked. Dewey was near the 'Cats goal.

Ted could see he was trying to help, but he was getting in Bucky's way. Bucky couldn't see the ball. If Dewey didn't move, a Tadpole might be able to—

"Score!" Stookie groaned. "I can't believe the Tadpoles scored on us so soon into the game." He turned to Ted. "If you had been back there, doing your job, we'd still be ahead! All I can say is, you better not ever try switching with me!"

Chapter 5

Ted felt bad about the goal. But as he jogged back into position, he decided he really couldn't be blamed for it. It wasn't his fault that Dewey had gotten in Bucky's way.

I bet if I'd made a goal Stookie would be singing a different tune, he thought. He tried not to think about how he'd run Stookie down. *Next time, I'll make it work,* he vowed.

He got his chance five minutes before the end of the first half. He found himself in the middle of the field with the ball. Ahead of him, Bundy was trying to get free of a Tad-pole defender.

Ted decided not to wait to see if Bundy got free. Instead, he dribbled upfield and yelled, "Bundy, switch!"

Bundy didn't hesitate. He dropped back. The Tadpole defender went with him. Except for the Tadpole fullbacks and goalie, there was nothing but open field in front of Ted!

Then Stookie appeared, running fast and far ahead of his defender. Ted heard pounding footsteps behind him as Bundy's defender charged him. Ted had no choice but to pass to Stookie.

Stookie caught the pass easily. He jerked to a stop to the right of the goal and slammed the ball into the net. The 'Cats were up 2–1.

"Nice assist," said Bundy as he jogged past Ted to his position.

"Thanks!" said Ted. He was pleased that his switch had worked so well, but still, he hadn't done what he'd really wanted to do.

Luckily, there's a whole other half left to go! he thought happily. He sucked on orange slices and drank a cup of water during halftime, all the while thinking about how surprised everyone would be when he scored his first goal.

The second half started. Ted waited impatiently for the chance to switch with one of the halfbacks. He followed the ball wherever it went, even when it meant moving out of his position. Twice more he switched positions with the halfbacks, once with Amanda, once with Bundy. Another time, he was so focused on the ball that he bumped into his sister.

"Hey, watch it!" she cried, rubbing her shoulder. "What's with you? You're all over the field today!"

Ted ignored her. But he soon found out she wasn't the only one who'd noticed his getting out of position. During a break in play, he felt a tap on his shoulder.

"Ted, I'm subbing in for you," said Edith "Eddie" Sweeny. "Coach wants to talk to you."

Ted's stomach sank as he ran to the bench. He took a seat near the coach. "Uh, Eddie said you wanted to talk to me?"

The coach watched the action on the field for a moment and then said, "You looked like you could use a break. You've been pretty busy out there today. Sit back, and take it easy." That was all.

Ted breathed a sigh of relief. He'd thought the coach was going to tell him to stop switching positions. It turned out he just wanted Ted to get a rest—which he needed anyway! But as he reached for a cup of water, he saw the coach look at him with a slight frown.

Chapter 6

As the second half continued, other players subbed in for the starters. Ted wished he'd be put back in, but the game ended with him still on the bench.

The 'Cats won, 5–1. Ted felt good knowing his assist had helped their score. For the first time in days, he was friendly to his sister, even helping her find a misplaced shin pad.

Their mother had been at the game, but she had to stop at the grocery store on the way home. The twins decided to walk home instead of going with her.

They hadn't gone more than a block when they heard footsteps running up behind them. It was Stookie.

"What were you trying to prove out there?" he demanded, staring at Ted.

Ted stopped. "What do you mean?" he asked.

"You know what I mean," Stookie said angrily. Before Ted could respond, Stookie added, "You're a fullback, Ted. Usually you're a good one, but today, sheesh! It was like you were hoping the coach would put you in as a halfback. If I didn't know better, I would have said you were even trying to take over my position!" He barked out a short laugh. "Well, I've got news for you. There's no way you're getting my position, bud. In fact, you'll be lucky to keep your own position with the way you were playing today!" With that, Stookie spun on his heel and stormed away.

Ted turned, open-mouthed, to Lisa. She was looking at him thoughtfully.

"What?" he said. "You think I was lousy to-day, too?"

Lisa shrugged.

Ted blurted, "I was just doing what the coach taught us in practice! And it worked, too, didn't it? I made an assist for the first time in my life! But did anyone care about that? No! They were too busy cheering for Stookie and his stupid goal." Fighting back tears, Ted took off down the street, leaving Lisa to stare after him.

Chapter 7

Ted didn't say much at dinner that night. Mrs. Gaddy and Lisa, on the other hand, talked about the game all through the meal, filling Mr. Gaddy in on what he'd missed.

"Oh, and you should have seen Ted!" Mrs. Gaddy said with pride. "You made an assist, didn't you?"

Ted nodded, feeling a little spark of pleasure at the memory.

"I don't think I've ever seen you dribble that far downfield during a game before,"

Mrs. Gaddy continued. "Why did you do it in this game? Was it a special play or something?"

Ted was about to explain about switching and his hopes of making a goal when he realized Lisa was watching him closely. Suddenly, he didn't feel like sharing his secret.

"Uh, no," he said quietly. "I—I just didn't see any open players on the field so I kept going." He turned his attention back to his dessert, hoping no one would see his red face. He finished as fast as he could, then excused himself. When he reached his bedroom, he closed the door and leaned against it.

Why didn't he want Lisa to find out his secret plan? Was it because he'd feel foolish if it didn't succeed? Or was he afraid she'd think it was silly that he wanted people to cheer for him?

"She wouldn't understand," he said out

loud. "People clap for her all the time. I just want a turn, that's all."

Later that night, Ted came into the kitchen looking for a snack. As he rummaged around in the pantry, he saw that the cordless phone wasn't in its cradle. That's when he heard Lisa whispering. She was standing in the hall-way, her back to Ted.

He held his breath and listened.

"Great, so you'll talk to him about Ted's switching?" she murmured into the phone. "Thanks. Good night."

Before Ted could move, Lisa turned around and saw him standing there. A look of alarm crossed her face.

"What was that all about?" Ted asked, nar-rowing his eyes.

"N—nothing!" Lisa stammered. She hung up the phone and disappeared up the stairs before Ted could quiz her further.

Ted looked at the phone. An idea struck him. He picked up the receiver and hit the redial button. In another moment, Ted would know whom his sister had been talking to.

"Hello, this is the Neel residence. Bundy speaking."

Ted quietly hung up the phone without saying a word.

Chapter 8

Ted lay awake in bed that night, wondering about Lisa's phone call.

Bundy was the captain of the team. One of his responsibilities was to talk to the coach about team problems.

So if Lisa asked Bundy to talk to the coach about my switching, Ted thought, *then she thinks it's a problem. Why would she think that?*

He sat up. *She must have guessed my secret! And I'll just bet she doesn't want me to get the chance to make a goal!*

He flopped back down in the bed. "Man,

my own sister, out to get me," he said to the darkness. "I don't believe it."

Yet the more he thought about it, the more it seemed like the only explanation possible.

Ted didn't sleep well that night. When he got up the next morning, he was grumpy. When he saw Lisa, his mood darkened even more.

So you decided to ruin my plans, huh? he thought angrily. *Well, two can play at that game.*

Halfway through breakfast Lou Barnes called to see if the twins wanted to meet him at the town pool. Mrs. Gaddy gave her permission.

Ted and Lisa hurried to get their swim gear together. Ted finished first and went back downstairs.

"Ted, could you grab my pool pass from the kitchen drawer?" Lisa called from her room.

Ted didn't answer. He pulled the drawer

open and rummaged through the pens, pencils, and other junk until he found the envelope with the pool passes. He stuck the one with his name on it in his pocket. After a moment's hesitation, he slid the others back into the envelope and closed the drawer.

Mrs. Gaddy dropped them off at the pool five minutes later. Ted showed his pass to the guard, who waved him through. Ted started toward the locker room.

"Hey, wait!" said Lisa. "Where's my pass?"

Ted looked at her innocently. "Didn't you bring it?" he asked.

"No! I asked you to get it for me! Didn't you hear me?"

Ted shook his head. The guard shrugged. "Sorry, miss, but I can't let you in without a pass. Pool rules."

"Aww, too bad, Lisa." Ted tried not to see the disappointed look on Lisa's face as she slumped into a chair outside the gate.

* * *

Later that day, Ted decided to walk to the library. There was a new book on spaceships he wanted to check out.

On his way there, he passed Lisa on her bike. When she learned where he was going, she asked him to pick up a book for her. "It's the next one in this series I'm reading about girl adventurers," she said.

Ted found the book he wanted at the library and sat reading it for half an hour. Then he checked it out and started for home. He hadn't even bothered looking for Lisa's book.

"Oops, I forgot," he said when she asked him for it later. He felt a twinge of guilt, but tried to ignore it.

Lisa gave him a funny look, but didn't say anything.

After dinner, however, she finally exploded. The twins had heard the tune of the ice-cream truck and knew it was heading to their street. They were allowed to get a treat but had to pay for it with their own money. Ted had a dollar in his pocket, but Lisa had to run upstairs to her piggy bank.

"Ask the ice-cream man to wait for me, okay?" she hollered. But when she ran out into the yard, clutching her dollar, all she saw was the back of the truck as it turned out of their neighborhood.

She turned to Ted, who was calmly licking his treat.

"What's gotten into you today?" she said, fighting back tears. "You've been mean to me all day!"

When Ted didn't answer, Lisa ran into the house.

"See if I ever do anything nice for you again," Ted thought he heard her say.

Chapter 9

For the second night in a row, Ted didn't sleep well. The image of Lisa crying because of something he'd done made him feel rotten. He woke up the next morning determined to apologize for having been so mean.

He changed his mind, however, when he saw her talking with Bundy before the game against the Torpedoes. The two glanced at Ted from time to time. He was sure they were talking about him.

Lisa and Bundy broke apart a moment later. Bundy walked toward Ted.

Ted half-expected Bundy to lecture him about staying in position, or to tell him that he'd talked to the coach about Ted's problem. But Bundy just punched him on the shoulder and wished him a good game. Then he walked up to Stookie and started talking to him.

Maybe the coach is going to talk to me instead, Ted thought nervously. But no one said anything to him during warm-up drills. Coach Bradley put him in at his usual position at the start of the game.

Ted began to wonder if he might have misunderstood Lisa's phone call. *But if she wasn't asking Bundy to talk to the coach, then who did she ask him to talk to?*

He didn't have time to think of an answer. The Torpedoes were bearing down on them with full force.

The Torpedo right striker had the ball. She dodged around Amanda and kept coming. Ted thought she was heading straight for the goal.

Bucky seemed to think so, too. He came out of the goal to challenge her.

In a flash, the Torpedo kicked the ball to her teammate who was right at the goal mouth. Bucky was too far out of the goal to stop a kick. It looked like the Torpedoes would score first.

But just as the Torpedo connected with the ball, Ted leaped into the goal. The ball soared toward him, chest high. Ted made sure he didn't use his arms or hands. Instead, he stopped the ball with his chest. It rebounded off him and bounced away from the goal. Lisa quickly got control of it and sent it down the sideline.

The fans went wild.

"Great save!" Lisa crowed.

"Thanks!" said Ted. He took a deep breath. "Listen, about yesterday—"

He was interrupted when Bucky slapped him on the back. "Hey, I thought you were supposed to yell 'Switch!' when you wanted to change positions!" Bucky said with a laugh.

Ted looked at him sharply. *Is Bucky making fun of me?*

No, he decided. *Bucky was just making a joke.*

Ted didn't have time to wonder why Lisa's face was bright red. The ball was coming their way again.

Chapter 10

Ted, Lisa, and the other fullbacks got into position. The Torpedoes passed the ball back and forth, then slowly closed in on the goal.

The right striker had the ball again. She glanced at her center and the center started toward the goal.

She's going to pass to him! Ted realized. Without hesitation, he rushed into the open space between them just as the right striker kicked a pass to the middle. Ted was there to steal the ball. There was nothing in front of him but open space.

He started to dribble. A quick glance showed him that both Bundy and Dewey were covered. Amanda was too far away to pass to. He kept dribbling.

"Ted, switch!"

It was Bundy! Ted faltered a step, then kept going. Bundy's defender, confused, followed Bundy back to Ted's position before realizing what had happened. By that time, Ted had crossed the center line.

Ted's heart was pounding. He could see the 'Cat strikers trying to get free for a pass. But the Torpedo defense was just too tough.

"Ted, switch!"

Stookie was the one who made the call this time. Ted dribbled madly past his teammate. The only thing between him and the goal were the fullbacks!

But unlike Bundy's defender, Stookie's

defender didn't follow Stookie. Instead, he moved in on Ted. Ted knew he had to act fast or lose the ball. With a mighty effort, he stopped, planted one foot on the ground, and kicked with all his strength.

Ted held his breath. The ball soared in the air, over the heads of the fullbacks, straight toward the goal—

Clang!

It hit the goal post and bounced straight up into the air. Ted couldn't believe it. He'd missed!

A blur of movement caught his eye. Stookie was rushing forward, his defender a step behind. When the ball fell, he headed it into the goal. Score! A second later, the ref blew his whistle to end the first half.

"Yes!" Ted cried, pumping his fist in the air. "Way to go, Stookie!"

Stookie grinned, but shook his head. "You're the one who deserves the credit for that goal!

There's no way the ball would have been down here if it weren't for you."

Ted was grabbed in a bear hug from behind. It was Lisa.

Stookie said, "Actually, Lisa deserves some thanks, too. After all, she's the one who asked Bundy to talk to me about switching with you sometime. Too bad you didn't make the goal like you wanted. Well, maybe next time!"

Ted stared at Stookie in amazement. Then he turned to Lisa. She was grinning happily.

"How'd you guess?" he said.

"We're twins," she answered simply. "I just put myself in your place and figured out what you were trying to do last game. Plus I saw the way you looked when the coach told his switching story." She leaned in and whispered, "Stookie needed a little convincing, is all. Hope you don't mind that I asked Bundy to talk to him."

Ted gave his sister a hug. "You're the best,"

he whispered. "I'm sorry about being so mean yesterday. Can I make it up to you?"

Just then, they heard a melody being played in the distance.

"You sure can make it up to me," Lisa said as they headed off the field together. "After the game, you chase down that ice-cream truck and buy me whatever I want!"